CW00759102

ACCIDENTAL
CROSSING

Accidental Crossing
Copyright © 2023 by Laura Barnett

All rights reserved. No part of this book may be reproduced or
transmitted in any form or by any means without written permission
from the publisher and author.

Additional copies may be ordered from the publisher for educational,
business, promotional or premium use.
For information, contact ALIVE Book Publishing at:
alivebookpublishing.com, or call (925) 837-7303.

Interior design by Alex P. Johnson
Book Cover by C.J. Swanston

ISBN 13
978-1-63132-198-6

Library of Congress Control Number: 2023902254
Library of Congress Cataloging-in-Publication Data
is available upon request.

First Edition

Published in the United States of America by ALIVE Book Publishing
an imprint of Advanced Publishing LLC
3200 A Danville Blvd., Suite 204, Alamo, California 94507
alivebookpublishing.com

PRINTED IN THE UNITED STATES OF AMERICA

10 9 8 7 6 5 4 3 2 1

ACCIDENTAL CROSSING

Laura Barnett

ABOOKS
Alive Book Publishing

Dedicated to my mom, Colleen "Coco" Elam, and my mother-in-law, Louise "Lou" Barnett.

Chapter One

LOLO AND MAX

Max and I live in a small village. It is partnered with a prideful mountainous region that circles the village with a protection that is appreciated by the townspeople. It snows most of the year which is intriguing and inviting for those who love the village and have stayed for many generations. The younger ones are on skis early, usually by two or three years old. Our village is in a remote area inhabited by a mix of personalities that includes shy, chatty, and very loud.

Everyone believes in understanding and compassion for one another. It is often said that the folks of our village have a positive energy that floats to the mountain tops, forms a circle in halo fashion, and protects everyone under it.

I adopted Max and was overwhelmed to be picked out of several potential guardians. All the guardians had been interviewed and I was the lucky one. I remember the outline of his sturdy little face as he was brought down the small curvy path leading to my house. I watched out the window as the adoption representative, known as Allie, exited the car.

"Hi Lolo, we made it!" Allie said to me with so much enthusiasm in her voice that it sounded like a shout. She knew I would be standing by the front window; she knew how much I wanted to adopt from all our previous meetings. Allie carefully took Max out of the small seat in the back of the car. He had a fuzzy light-colored blanket adorned with tiny stars wrapped around his shoulders. The moments leading up to this miraculous occasion wound up my internal mommy clock so fast that I was trying to settle myself in a way that would not alarm Max. I waited many years for this day and little fireworks were bursting in my heart that made tears come to my eyes.

In my village, there were other parents waiting for an opportunity to adopt but few children were available or in need. We were the only village out of hundreds, chosen because of its proximity to an elite school. The school that treated all the kids like their own, where learning was an adventure, and now was the time for me to make a difference in a child's life. To guide a young soul to enjoy all the village and I could offer, to be a guardian angel for sweet Max.

Max was giggling at first glance, and his bubbly one-year-old cherub face looked like crying he had so much joy in his heart. My face felt tingly. This long-awaited day was finally in my lap. I remember his belly laugh and reflecting on it always brings me to squeeze my palms into a fist-saluting thank you to the universe. I made a promise to myself to always look after him, keep him safe, and allow his little soul to flourish to the highest level possible.

During the first few years, Max and I spent many nights under the stars in our backyard patio. It was perfectly positioned to see the night sky, facing west of the trees. Looking at our village from the top of the highest mountain, the houses were lined with a precision and order that did not seem to be real. The small huts each had the same number of lights. Most evenings, a community twinkle would light up and embrace the neighborhood to everyone's delight. Perhaps this close-knit community helped Max flourish. I was always reading to Max, mostly about astronomy, which was my favorite subject, one that I had studied for years. I taught Max a lot in his early years about the many galaxies in the universe.

Max would always say, "Mom, I want to travel in space when I am older and visit all the galaxies!"

By the time Max was seven, he had been on his small skis for a good amount of time, enjoying the safety and proximity of the village and its school. Max was a bit of a daredevil, which always kept me on my toes. His school afforded privileges for the younger skiers to access what was known as Recess Ridge. Instead of taking the school break on the playground, the children could opt to ski on Recess Ridge. Kids of all ages would journey up the mountain by chairlift and, depending on their age, would be able to get off at a designated elevation before making the downhill trip.

Beautiful gigantic 100-foot robust trees waved at the skiers as they sailed through the powdery snow. The trees would sneeze fresh snow, inviting giggles and high fives. You could hear birds practicing sweet sounds in a tight pitch that sounded confident and curious in the fresh air. At times Max would say, "Mom, this must be heaven."

The recess allowed just enough time for Max and his schoolmates to make it part way up the ridge and feel the rush as they glided back in time for class. The buzz around school was the top of the ridge was reserved for the graduating seniors. No one was allowed at the very top except a select handful of teachers during the school year or the seniors who were participating in a special winter camp.

One day I received a message from Max's homeroom teacher, Miss Sweets. She wanted to speak with me right away. We arranged to meet in her office before school was dismissed.

"Hi Lolo," Miss Sweets said sporadically before she even turned around after I entered her office.

Miss Sweets was not her name; I had heard from the other parents she wanted the kids to have a kind impression of her and not be intimidated. She was, after all, a very large woman with a walk that sounded more like a stomp. To her credit, she had eyes that seemed to exude forgiveness even if none was needed.

Miss Sweets was silent for a few awkward moments before saying, "I am concerned about Max."

This was followed with a predictable deep breath that she seemed to enjoy taking her time doing. This was not the first teacher conference for me. I had other conferences with different teachers, but this one was different. She made a gesture for me to sit down when all the other times with teachers we stood in the hallway casually chatting.

"The other day we had recess as scheduled, and Max was asked to stay on the playground because Recess Ridge was closed due to a heavy snowfall. I know the playground is not as fun, and it was difficult to keep twenty-five kids busy for the entire forty-five minutes. Once recess was over, I did a headcount, and we could not find Max. After several minutes of looking, we found him on the roof of the school on the North side which is closer to the mountain. I have no idea how he got up there."

Miss Sweets went on to say that Max had excelled in his studies over the past year and was at the top of his class.

"I just don't know how to keep him challenged. Although he is only seven, I am worried that if I don't offer him more challenges, I will be holding him back. He is an exceptional child. We have never had a student like him."

I felt a pulse of fear and pride swirling around me.

The two feelings were competing and eventually canceled each other out, leaving me with a blank look on my face. For a few moments, Miss Sweets could not get out what she wanted to say as if trying to change her mind and address a different incident that might occur.

"I want to suggest something," Miss Sweets said at last, in a confident manner.

"I have met with the other teachers and all the higher ups. We have an idea but need your permission."

Miss Sweets went on to describe winter camp that is designed to last two weeks. It is reserved for older children, and the youngest they ever had was eleven years old. However, due to the signs of incredible physical and academic abilities Max was showing, they felt the winter camp could help him move up to a more advanced classroom in the spring. After all, the camp had graduating seniors and was a good mix for beginners.

As Sweets was speaking, I felt badly that Max had scared her and the other teachers, but I also knew this conversation would be coming sooner rather than later. Max had shared with me on several occasions how bored he felt at school. I agreed to let him go to the winter camp hoping it would give him the additional support he needed. After all, I was a single guardian and Max had no other siblings. The camp could be just what he needed. At the dinner table that evening, Max was thrilled to find out the news from my conversation with Miss Sweets.

"That is so awesome Mom!" Max said with a smile that melted my heart.

The joy of this exciting news resonated for days with both of us. Earlier in the school year, Max had heard many stories about the winter camp from his classmates who had older siblings. Stories that included wild ski rides that only the bravest would dare to try. Max also heard he could learn things about the universe, important things that were only taught at camp. Max was so overjoyed he could barely sleep, waking up several times to open the back door and peek at the open sky. He did this whenever he felt excitement about something. The blast of fresh air mixed with the visual of the open sky was calming.

Max had a collection of twenty-three rocks shaped like stars. We would get them out on the weekends and make patterns on our front porch.

Max would say, "Mom, I want to shine bright someday, as bright as the shiniest."

I remember saying, "Max, you are my shiniest star."

Max would always give me a smug smile and say, "Oh Mom!"

Max slept with all twenty-three of his stars that night and placed them in a circle around his bed. He would tell me this is what he did on special occasions when he wanted to get the attention of the universe. Max said it was easier to talk with the galaxy when his stars were in perfect alignment.

The next day at recess, Max told me he quickly took the lift to the ridge and screamed with joy as loudly as he could all the way back down. I pictured my small child with exceptional abilities laughing his laugh that could be mistaken as a cry, his joy gliding down the hill and through the trees, his breath feeling as powerful as the wind and creating bursts of snow falling off any branch he passed. In hindsight, I must admit I had not known everything about the winter camp and, if I had, I would never have allowed Max to attend.

Chapter Two

WINTER CAMP

"**M**orning ski campers! My name is Scottie, and I am going to lead this group for the next two weeks. The most important thing to remember is to listen to all instructions I give you and, above all, have a great time! You will have rigorous academic studies every morning. In the afternoon, we will have games and select ski courses you will be allowed to use. There is one ski jump that is off limits to all twenty-five of you. Graduate Hill is reserved for the graduates. The graduates have participated in Winter Camp for several years and have been selected with great honors to graduate to their next journey and educational assignment. We can talk about this later. Just remember it is off limits."

Max was fidgety. He was listening to Scottie who had deep blue eyes that twinkled in the reflection of the sun, and this was distracting Max. However, his biggest distraction was thinking of Graduate Hill. He wanted to go there and see what it was all about. After the first few days, Max continued to feel restless. He enjoyed his studies. Although scaled down for the younger group, it was challenging work as the teachers had promised. He had fun in the afternoon playing snow games, even making up a few obstacle courses with his friends. Nonetheless, something kept tugging at him-he could not go to the "off-limits" slope. After all, everyone back home including his mom made such a big deal about his special talents, especially on the slopes.

No one told him Winter Camp would have a secret slope where he would not be allowed. Max decided he would pester his camp counselor, Scottie.

"Please Scottie, I just want to peek. Can I go to the top and just watch when the graduates are practicing?"

Scottie replied, "No Max, it is not your turn. Those who are not graduates must not go to the top of the mountain. You will thank me later my daredevil friend. Besides, I am not exactly sure what happens at the top, and I am your counselor!"

Max put up such a fuss that the other kids started to stare. He was not saying anything in response to Scottie, just banging a ski against a fence, pretending he was trying to get off excess snow, but it was obvious to all he was mad.

Suddenly he blurted, "It's not fair that I cannot see what the more advanced kids are doing. How will I ever improve? Why did I even come here?!"

"Max, you have a lot to learn before you can have a turn, please trust me. When the time is right, I am sure you will receive an invitation. You must be a lot older to graduate, and there are so many more ski camps you need to complete in order to qualify."

Max seemed to understand but felt this could not be farther from the truth.

The next day Max was out of sorts. Graduate Hill looked different this day. It was tall and proud as always, but the fog that generally lifted by mid-day was still lingering. The mountain was half covered with what looked like a heavy blanket, as if nursing a fever. Max had not slept much the night before, tossing and turning, imagining how he could prove everyone wrong. He felt convinced he was ready for the off-limits slope. Even opening his cabin door to get a burst of fresh air and peek at the night sky did not seem to help with his restlessness.

Max was innocently stubborn, as any seven-year-old could be. He decided to come up with a clever plan, one he thought would be just a little outside the rules, not enough to fully break them, but just enough to satisfy his brave curiosity. After all, he knew he would be invited back for the next several years and could not stand the thought of someone asking him about Graduate Hill without something to tell.

The more he thought about his plan and his goal, the more it made sense to him. He knew he had to peek, just a small peek at what was going on so he could practice for when he was invited one day.

Scottie asked the group to split up according to their bracelet color. Yellow for the younger, blue for the intermediates, and green for the advanced or graduates. Just as Max was heading for his group, he motioned with his hand for Scottie to come over.

"Hey Scottie, can I go back to the bunks and lie down? I don't feel great."

Max stared at Scottie as if to challenge him to say no to a sick kid. He even snuck in a small groan for good measure.

"Ok, I will send someone to check on you shortly. Now go straight to the cabins and feel better, Max. Counselors are in the cafeteria so be sure to let them know you are not feeling well. They will call for a nurse."

Max started down the hill, on his small skis that seemed to elevate him to anywhere he decided to go. This day, he wanted to spy on Graduate Hill, and he promised himself he would be oh, so careful. It would be a secret he could tell his friends back home during a Recess Ridge break, and

Max could not stop smiling. He felt better than ever. He swerved before the last exit by a gate that would have taken him to the cabins. By now he was not in close view. He avoided the lift to Graduate Hill as that was way too risky. Someone would surely see him. He decided to take off his skis in order to hike up the hill under the trees that are parallel to the ski lift, giving him the best chance to go undetected.

The trees were like a curtain for his small self, and he felt temporarily protected and comforted. The longer branches seemed to be on his side. He imagined the trees saying,

"We can hide you, you got this!"

As Max got closer, he started to feel anxious and needed to calm himself down. In his mind he called on his mom. She would understand his curiosity more than anyone else. He thought about his favorite shiny star that he kept in his pocket. It was his lucky star his mom would tell him. Max took out his star and held it tightly. The comfort of the star coupled with getting closer to the top was overwhelming and exciting. He told himself he was amazed by his cleverness. He replayed in his mind the many school yard tricks and Recess Ridge shenanigans. Max settled into a hiding spot with a low branch covering him as if this day were rehearsed. Max with his shiny star, perfectly placed in his left hand, squeezed one more time. Not knowing at first if he is in the exact right spot, his eyes seemed to play tricks on him. He blinked as if snowflakes obstructed his view for just a few seconds. He looked more carefully and saw bright green lights all around a bunch of kids, the seniors of the camp. Max was nervous someone would see him but had to get closer. It was a special celebration, and the music was magnetic. It sounded like angels were singing and the light around all the graduates beamed so brightly he could barely see them.

Max got as close as he could without being detected and saw a line of about ten graduates all waiting to go down the special ski jump that was off limits. It was very steep. The snow continued to fall and obstruct his view slightly. A counselor was talking to each person and putting something around their neck in a ceremonious way. Max could not tell what the graduates were saying to each other. They were laughing and seemed happy and prideful.

Max grew impatient. The entire point of getting to the top was to see what type of ski jumps the graduates were doing. There were few trees to hide him so that he could get closer undetected, look down the slope to see what the challenge was, and decide if he could do it. Max made up his mind to do something very bold. He would take this opportunity to show the graduates in line a few tricks while they were waiting for their turn. Max pictured doing all the amazing flips and turns he was used to doing back home. Naturally, the graduates would clap and cheer. He would try to get closer to the first person in line to take a quick peek at where the hill was going. All of this sounded perfect, and the temptation was too great. He could not resist. He imagined Scottie apologizing, saying he made a mistake and that he should have been with the other graduates today.

As Max left the comfort of his hiding spot, the snow stopped for just a minute. He noticed a teacher he did not recognize. She was taller than the average teacher and seemed to be glowing softly. Her gentle features captivated Max for just a few seconds and he noticed she was handing out what looked like a small book to everyone in line. The books were tiny, yet the light reflecting off them was almost blinding.

Max started to feel left out. He was the youngest student to ever get an invite to the winter camp. He was special so why could he not get a book from someone who looked like an angel? Max felt it was time to make a move, his biggest move ever. He needed to do something grand at the winter camp. What if he could pull off the most amazing tricks to wow the seniors? The line for the ski jump started at the top, and it wrapped partially down the slope before the launch. Max decided he would go to the top of the slope for just a few tricks. He would then take a bow. Max had to walk behind the few trees that were the backdrop of the slope so no one could stop him before his big debut.

Backflips were his specialty; he always got an, "Oh my gosh that is amazing Max" from all ages back at home. Max started to go faster and faster down the slope towards the front of the line. He realized a little too late that he could not slow down. As if he was being sucked down. He felt immobilized and unable to do any flips. As he got close to the front of the line, he **accidentally** bumped into a boy who was waiting his turn and knocked him out of place. The book he was holding went flying. The other kids and teachers started shouting, slow down, come back! Max was spinning out of control. The slope was steep indeed, and as he made his descent, it suddenly became very dark. Max held on to the belief that even if he did not do his special tricks, he must have impressed everyone. The expression on everyone's face must have been priceless, he chuckled quietly.

Max was now going even faster down a dark tunnel. He braced for impact. His curly brown hair was swirling around his face with his wide green eyes. Surely, he would end up at the bottom of the hill and his counselors would come get him. He might be in trouble but enjoyed the rush.

He felt a little guilty about bumping a graduate out of line, but accidents happen.

Max started to see beautiful rainbow colors. It was unimaginable what he felt and could see. He knew he might not remember it all and started to feel tired. The colors faded and he fell fast asleep.

Scottie got word Max was missing and headed straight for Graduate Hill. There was so much chaos going on and Max was nowhere to be found. This had never happened before, ever.

The counselors knew Max had crossed to a galaxy he knew nothing about and the graduate due for this journey who had prepared for years was accidentally knocked out of line. It would take Max somewhere that was unknown and unfamiliar. It would be very hard to get him back.

Chapter Three

LANE

Lane peeked out her front curtains to see what all the noise was about. Her small face partially in view. It sounded like a delivery truck was circling the cul-de-sac of her apartment complex as if lost. The truck looked too large to be jamming around in such a small space of a street.

She was alone today, just as she was most days except for her fluffy Pomeranian dog, Sasha. Lane was always with Sasha. She had a special medical card to take Sasha in stores and if she wanted to travel, which she did not, she could take Sasha with her on any train, plane, or bus. Her doctor had suggested the medical card. Her recent miscarriage was devastating and since Lane was not sleeping very well, he also prescribed her pills which made her feel like a zombie, but at least she could get out of bed.

Lane trusted Sasha, a connection she cherished more than ever during this difficult time. Sasha's pink collar was full of bling and sparkled more than Lane on most days.

"An old dog with a hip collar," her sister Cassie would say.

Lane was kind. She had rosy cheeks that gave her soft features and the appearance she was wearing makeup, but that was not something she preferred. She carried herself well.

"As if that were a thing," her sister, Cassie, would always say with a chuckle.

The sound of the delivery truck became louder and

sounded in need of a new muffler. The delivery truck finally found the spot where it could stop with only a partial inconvenience to a few driveways. It made Lane more nervous, or maybe it was the medication, nothing was in full focus for her. Lane paused for a second, almost confused about what to do, she turned and looked at Sasha.

"Sasha be quiet."

Sasha stopped her squeaky bark for just a second and gave a knowing look and then continued as if competing with the truck with no muffler.

Lane wanted to sit comfortably on the couch with her head tilted back and re-play the dream she had the night before, over and over. Reliving the dream brought her comfort. She dreamt of a little boy needing her to come to him right away.

He kept saying, "Mommy, Mommy."

She could only hear the voice; she could not see the child. Lane wondered, what if this little boy was her miscarried child? What if he was looking for her? Lane remembered the distant, almost desperate calls for "Mommy," and the feeling he was in the baby's room she had prepared for a child that did not come. The noise was not the loud hum of a delivery truck anymore, it was a persistent knock on the front door.

"How can I help you?" Lane said curtly without opening the door.

"Ma'am, I need your signature for this delivery."

"Just a minute," Lane said and quickly put Sasha in the bathroom next to the front entrance so she could sort out this delivery business. As she opened the door ever so slightly, she was handed a tablet to sign and noticed the delivery man was not making eye contact. He was wearing a headset listening to music, perhaps thinking about his next stop.

Maybe he could not see her. Lane was used to feeling small in the world but now she felt invisible. He snatched the tablet back. She hoped he would at least gesture he got the tablet, and she would be sure he knew she was a real person. That did not happen. As she looked at the oversized box more carefully, she noticed a picture of a baby crib, which immediately made her stomach turn. As Lane opened her mouth trying to yell "take it back," the delivery man was already in his truck releasing the parking brake.

The picture of the crib was a beautiful masterpiece that looked more like a small carriage.

The crib was back-ordered months ago; the last piece that would unite a child's room. A room that was already filled with an easy chair, a small rocking horse, and gentle colors spilling down every corner in rainbow fashion.

There was a nook under the window with several stuffed animals sitting as if at attention. Lastly, a tiny bookshelf with books that would not make sense to a baby until much older. Mostly classics for adults but Lane was determined to read anything good to her new baby as often as she could.

At one time, the nursery was a slice of heaven to Lane. She would visit the room often, and it was "beyond dreams and blue skies" her sister would say. It was a chance for Lane to give a child an opportunity to have an amazing life. A life very different from the one she had lived as a child.

Lane left the crib in its big box outside on her porch. It was too heavy for her to move and what good would it do to put it together. Her "due date" was now officially canceled. She placed an old, dark-colored sheet over the box so that she would not see the crib picture each time she left the house. It was not blocking the front entrance, so it seemed the covered-up box had found a temporary home to the left of her front door. It was a corner of the front porch that never saw light and now the crib would linger in this corner of darkness for who knew how long. It was a darkness she understood.

Lane retrieved Sasha; her precious little dog demanded to know what was going on. Instead of squeaky barking she switched to incessant panting. It was time for their morning routine of walking to the local coffee shop, Mo's, five blocks away. Most days Lane would walk by a few neighbors who huddled together, giving her disapproving glances. Lane was used to being on the outside. She would walk around the group of ladies whispering, wishing she could just hop a fence somewhere to avoid them, but it was not possible. The ladies were not really saying hello and not exactly ignoring her. They simply exuded an obvious phoniness. Lane wore her slippers to Mo's. She usually had a bandana on her head to keep out the wind or cold but even on hot days lately she ended up wearing her slippers and bandana during the morning walk to Mo's.

Lane packed a small bag for Sasha with a portable water bowl and a tiny blanket. They made their way out the door and, fortunately, Lane did not see any neighbors. She breathed a deep sigh of relief.

Lane finally made the short walk to Mo's, a home away from home. The owner of Mo's always gave Sasha a dog biscuit once coffee was ordered. The community newspaper was generally available in one of the racks. It was not mainstream reporting, just for the townspeople. Lane looked forward to reading it, reading about local events she would never consider going to, but the thought was intriguing.

Mo's coffee shop was the anchor in her mornings. It was inside an old, renovated house that was decorated with couches and lamps and more couches. The outside was the highlight, Lane would always tell Cassie. Today it was adorned with beautiful yellow flowers that attracted hummingbirds and white butterflies, a surprising delight. A dance that was orchestrated to reveal the lightness and beauty to all who could see it. A lot of comforts inside and out gave off the vibe of visiting family.

Lane briefly took off her sunglasses before entering Mo's, feeling it was more respectful. She did her usual stride to the back patio to get Sasha settled before ordering her usual coffee. It seemed her favorite outside couch was always available, dumb luck she would tell Cassie. Lane was settled and it was time to look at the weekly newspaper to see what others were up to or planned on doing.

Lane knew she would not go to the local events, but it helped perk up her day imagining she would attend an opera or a local play. She could picture families going together or friends, dressed up and excited. Even before the miscarriage, Lane seemed to have a cloud over her. As Lane looked at the first page, there was an unusual looking ad that caught her attention.

"Have you ever miscarried a child? Do you feel sad or depressed? You may be experiencing a unique form of Post-Traumatic Stress Disorder (PTSD). Dr. Beck can help you through your journey of loss. She has a medical degree and is a trained metaphysical specialist."

Lane furrowed her brows in deep contemplation. Her thoughts were paralyzing, wondering whether she should be excited or confused. Someone was advertising to help women like her get through grief. Could this really be true?

She knew she needed to call her sister Cassie, her closest confidant and only sibling. Lane could not wait to call Cassie, so she pulled out her cell phone from her jacket pocket praying Cassie would pick up. On the last ring, she did.

"Cassie, you will not believe it. I'm at Mo's, reading an ad in the local paper. A doctor has taken interest in women who have had a miscarriage."

Cassie was silent for a few moments, trying to decipher what she was hearing. It was the pause Lane knew well, one that only happened when Cassie was not approving of what she was hearing but searched for a polite way to respond.

"Well, that's a little bit strange. Why are you interested? Other than the fact you have barely left your house or talked to anyone for weeks. Ok, sorry. Tell me more."

Cassie was more practical than Lane and had a unique way of figuring things out. Her brain was like a computer; input, analyze, and report. Lane depended on her for this and now, with the miscarriage, Lane felt lost. Cassie was her only family support since their mom died, but Cassie was not keen on making sense of dreams with spirits speaking or hearing a child calling for you. This type of thinking was always how Lane lived. She believed in spirits, talking to others who had passed on, and the supernatural. Cassie was married but Lane had never tied the knot. Lane never really considered marriage, after a long search and a few heartbreaks, she immersed herself in getting a degree in engineering. Her career was productive, and she enjoyed having the financial security that was lacking in her childhood. Now in her early 30s, she felt defeated. Lane had taken a family psychology class and understood the problems of having a baby to fill a void in life, the worst kind of parenting. On the other hand, what if one had a lot of love to give and no partner? Lane spent weeks and finally picked out the best donor sperm she could find, good genes, nice looking, educated, and look what happened. No baby. Lane was not particularly attractive; she did not even really look like Cassie who could get any man, but she was smart. They were both smart.

"I am doing a little better and I didn't want to tell you this just yet. I am hearing a child, a boy calling me, nightly for the past week. He says 'Mommy, Mommy.' I wake up in the middle of the night and sometimes I walk to the baby's room. I keep hearing, 'It's me Max' and then I wake up. What if he is the spirit of the baby I miscarried? What if he is still around me, needing me?"

Lane's voice sounded higher pitched than usual. Cassie could tell she was struggling, and this kind of information also made her uncomfortable. She wanted her sister to be more logical, a simple request she wished Lane could hear. Lane continued,

"The night before last, I could hear him coughing in my dream. I think he is sick. You know I am intuitive about this kind of stuff. I think the baby is around me."

Lane was whispering now for fear someone at Mo's would hear her. Cassie was quiet for what seemed like a couple minutes, perhaps trying to process this new information with her computer brain.

"Wait a minute," said Cassie. "I thought you we're going to name your baby Oliver if a boy and Sophia if a girl."

"Cassie, I know but he keeps saying 'it's me Max' so maybe I would have named him Max. I think I should call Dr. Beck. She is not only a doctor, but she also believes in metaphysics. This must be a sign."

"Lane, please don't call her just yet. What if she is a quack? This is quite spontaneous, and you have never been a fan of counseling. God knows we both could have used it after Mom died. You should see if your dreams and voices settle down once you get through the loss of the baby. It's no secret this kind of trauma would make you more vulnerable to the types of dreams you are having. Perhaps your medications are influencing what you are hearing?"

"Cassie, the universe is trying to tell me something, and I need a professional to decode all of it. If I get a bad feeling during the first session, I promise I won't go back."

Cassie knew Lane was going to call Dr. Beck but wanted to at least slow her down with a little cautionary interference. As soon as Lane hung up with her sister, she gently nudged Sasha to get up so they could make the short walk home. Sasha woke up and did a tiny bark as if saying, "You woke me up from an amazing dream, shame on you!" Sasha then stared knowingly at Lane, as if giving the final approval.

Lane and Cassie's childhoods were difficult. Their mom married a crazy person when they were very young. He was and maybe still is an alcoholic. His name to Lane and Cassie was "Pets." They decided to spell Step in reverse one day. It was a day he was yelling at their dog, Chewy, who was the nicest dog. Chewy and their cat, Connie, were family pets, kinder than Pets. When their mother died unexpectedly, Lane and Cassie promised never to say his real name again because a name gave importance, and he was not important in their lives.

They had not heard from him in over fifteen years. Once their mom was gone, he was gone. Lane missed her mom now more than ever. Her mom was a saint in her eyes, always so kind and always there for her. Lane's mom would say to her when she was upset about Pets, "People don't change overnight but your perception of them can, pray for him." Lane never did, she held tightly to her hate.

They were teenagers when their mother died and lived with friends until they were able to go to college. Fortunately, they had a small inheritance which afforded them comforts.

"We aren't rich, but we are comfortable." Cassie would say to Lane when she would become stressed about money and the future. Cassie shut down after their mom died, not to Lane but to most of the world. She worked as a corporate executive as did her husband. Her husband was nice enough, but they both worked all the time.

Chapter Four

CALLING DR. BECK

Lane and Sasha entered the apartment. Lane wanted to find the most comfortable position to call Dr. Beck, and she started overthinking the entire experience. She had been depressed for weeks and questioned a strong dose of hope just by seeing an ad in a newspaper. Lane did not trust ordinary counselors. She thought talking with one would mean reliving unwanted childhood memories. But the word metaphysical sent a jolt of optimism through her body, putting her in a bind. She finally told herself that she would give very little information about her alcoholic stepfather, Pets. The focus would be on losing a baby and the dreams she was having. With that settled, she sat down and called Dr. Beck. She hoped to just leave a message for a doctor who must have many other patients.

The phone kept ringing and ringing and eventually Lane got a beep to leave a message. Whenever Lane got anxious, she would gently tug on her hair, using her fingers as a comb. Her hair felt brushed before she heard the beep. Lane took a very deep breath.

"Hello Dr. Beck, my name is Lane. I am calling you because I had a miscarriage several weeks ago, and I haven't been sleeping." Just saying those words caused Lane to feel emotional, making it hard for her to finish her sentence. Lane cleared her throat once more and stated that she looked forward to hearing from her.

Dr. Beck called back the very next day.

"Hi Lane, I would like to schedule our first visit, which is complimentary. I am emailing an extensive form you will need to complete prior to our meeting." Dr. Beck had a deep voice that was more businesslike than what Lane was expecting.

"OK, I would appreciate that. It has been difficult to get any sleep. Thank you so much." As Lane hung up the phone, she found it hard to believe she was the one talking to Dr. Beck. Saying "thank you so much" felt phony, almost contrived. Since her miscarriage, she had been observing her life and taking interesting notes but not feeling anything. Dr. Beck was not only a medical doctor but trained and believed in metaphysics, an interesting and, Lane felt, a promising combination. Lane kept reminding herself of this. Lane had had a miscarriage and felt a baby boy calling for her. How amazing that she could find someone who might understand her and help her connect the dots of her experiences.

The session was scheduled for the following week. As Lane placed the phone on the small round table by the door, she could not stop staring at her wilted plant in a colorless container. No matter how much she watered it or moved it around the apartment, it occupied her attention. All her other house plants were fake with a predictable stiffness, but her one wilted plant at least felt real to her. Even in a pathetic way. Lane contemplated this for some time before she started to fill out the online form Dr. Beck sent to her. Sasha was right by her side, wide eyed.

"Sasha, we are going to get help!"

Lane blurted this to Sasha as if she needed comfort. Sasha perked up, looked knowingly at Lane, and quickly fell back asleep.

The form had the usual questions and with trepidation Lane began to complete as much of it as she could in one sitting. Although she was filling out the form on the computer, Lane kept taking breaks, picking up her pen, twirling it full circle, scribbling, then pausing. It seemed the motion of the pen was triggering memories for her to continue whenever she got stuck on a question. The questionnaire went as follows.

GIVE A BRIEF SUMMARY
WHY YOU ARE SEEKING HELP:

I don't have any friends who are close enough to visit. My sister Cassie is my only family, and she lives far away. I was working but took a leave of absence once I found out I was pregnant. Unfortunately, I am no longer with child. I am taking the loss of the baby hard. I never considered I would miscarry a child as I am very healthy. The baby's room and even a college fund were in the start-up phase.

EXPLAIN ONE DREAM YOU HAD
RELATED TO YOUR MISCARRIAGE:

A week before my miscarriage, I dreamt someone was knocking at my front door. It is not loud at first but gets louder. I walk to the front door from my bedroom. As I open the front door, it's very quiet. It feels as if time has stopped and there is a darkness I cannot explain. I am scared. I remember a dark figure breathing, a labored breathing. I try to talk, scream, but nothing comes out of my mouth. The dark figure is carrying what looks like a swaddled baby as it moves past me to the baby's room. The figure bends over and places the swaddled baby on a chair. I try to move, but I am paralyzed. The baby is unraveled from its blanket. I look down and the baby is covered in blood. I try to scream, my mouth moves and, again, no sound.

EXPLAIN YOUR MISCARRIAGE:

I was with my sister, Cassie. She was visiting to help me get the final touches ready in the baby's room. We were watching a movie with Sasha, my dog. I have blocked out what movie we were watching, but I remember not feeling well. I went to bed early, leaving Sasha and Cassie to finish watching. I woke up in the middle of the night to go to the bathroom, what came out of me seemed unreal. As I was sitting on the toilet, I looked down between my legs, and I could see what looked like chunks of flesh coming out of me. It was confusing, and I assumed it wasn't good. I wondered why no one told me what it was like to have a miscarriage. Surely, I was losing the baby. Perhaps they didn't want to jinx me, but I wished I had known so the experience wasn't so frightening. I couldn't stop the bleeding, so I woke up Cassie. When I made the short walk to her room, Cassie screamed at the sight of blood on the floor. Blood was on the floor and everywhere on my pants.

As Lane was writing this down, memories flooded in that she did not think were any of Dr. Beck's business. Lane continued.

I remember Cassie screamed in a way that made me feel an intruder was in the house. I had heard her scream before but not like this. It made me mad that she screamed. I wanted her to be silent like me. I wanted her to watch what was happening as an observer and pretend with me that

nothing major was happening. Cassie grabbed several towels and we sat there. I with towels between my legs and she,
crying. The bleeding finally stopped, but now the baby was
in the toilet and not in the crib. I promised Cassie that night
I would never try again to have a baby. The baby high
turned to a toilet nightmare. I imagined Cassie saying, "Told
you so," but, of course, she didn't. Cassie never wanted to
have a baby after what we went through as children. Cassie
almost hated kids. She would say, "Kids are like rats trying
to get past lab experiments in order to survive the real
world."

Cassie was more analytical and did not feel emotions as
much as Lane. Lane felt weepy after filling out the online
form and considered deleting it and canceling her appointment. Her sister had made a good point. Questioning
whether this type of counseling was a good fit for her, if she
was desperate for help. Sure, she was suffering but she kept
it together most days. It was time to decide.

Lane took a deep breath. She knew she would never
change her mind. She took several deeper breaths and hit
the send button. She expected it would change the course of
her recovery in one way or another.

Chapter Five

COUNSELING

L ane was nervous at her first appointment. She sat quietly in an oversized chair in the front lobby of Dr. Beck's office. Her legs were crossed, and her hands tucked under on each side as if to keep warm. Lane was wearing her usual sweats outfit, convenient to wear around the house now that she was not working. Lane was not sure when she would return to work. She also liked the appearance a matching sweat outfit offered. It made it seem to the world she was on her way to the gym, an energy lacking in her life. Lane's only exercise now was taking Sasha to get coffee or food.

Lane could not keep her eyes off the beautiful print of a cypress tree directly in front of her, tall with exposed roots circling it. Some of the roots were more pronounced, which made them appear as if they were trying to breathe. A quiet suffocation that made Lane start to feel anxious. The frame imprisoned the tree, mirroring the current state of things for Lane who felt trapped in her own thoughts. Dr. Beck was late coming out. Lane waited several minutes before the door opened. A young woman was leaving in tears, she looked vaguely familiar. Lane said nothing, averting her eyes and feeling some of the young woman's embarrassment. Dr. Beck peeked out the door "Sorry I am late. I will be right with you."

Lane continued to stare at the cypress tree, a little startled by the crying woman but, then again, Dr. Beck specialized in post trauma from losing a baby. Of course, people will cry in counseling.

Dr. Beck opened the door after a few minutes and waved for Lane to come in. The room was tiny and, Lane thought, a bit messy for a therapist. There were papers and books scattered across her desk. It was odd there were no photos, degrees, or anything else on the walls. Dr. Beck had jet black hair with smooth brown skin and was attractive with a deep voice that made her seem masculine. Lane was staring without talking while trying to process the intensity of the young woman crying and the distinct look of Dr. Beck, feeling uncomfortable the whole time.

In the corner of her office there were two lounge chairs. Dr. Beck sat in one and asked Lane to sit across from her in the other.

"Lane, we can begin a treatment plan after today if we both feel it is a good fit."

Dr. Beck looked tired. Her hands were puffy even though she was not overweight. Lane pictured her drinking a lot of diet drinks, but how could Lane know and why would she care. Lane imagined she must be a good therapist, reading all those books to understand how her patients were feeling. Lane even visualized where she lived. A nice cottage with beautiful flowers all around and a white picket fence. A sense of comfort rained down on Lane and made an awkward situation more comfortable.

"OK Lane, let's get started." Dr. Beck said with a rubber band snap in her voice.

"I read your comments on the questionnaire. Thank you for being so open. I know you only want to focus on the miscarriage, but I need at least one story from your childhood that was either painful or scary. It may tie in. Close your eyes and relax. Now, think of the very first thing that comes to your mind."

Lane didn't have to think very hard about which story she would pull out of a hat. The defining story was crystal clear in her mind.

"I am four or five, dusting off my favorite coffee table. It is a coffee table I often hide under when I don't want anyone to know where I am. My sister Cassie is at school. My mom is in the kitchen, cleaning. She cleans all the time. Sometimes I help her do the dishes. She gets me a chair to stand on, but today I want to clean my favorite table with a duster that looks like a bunch of feathers stuck on a stick. My stepfather, whom I call Pets is home very early, and my mom is in a panic but I'm not sure why. She usually panics when he comes home late and wobbly, having a hard time opening the front door, even with a key. This is new. He is home early, and Mom is mad about it. It makes no sense to me. My mom says we must go as he is coming around to the front door. We need to leave out the back door, which leads to the garage. She yanks my arm to come with her quickly, and we jump into our faded blue station wagon. I am with her in the front seat, but I can barely see what's going on. Pets finally got the key to open the front door and can't find us. He comes into the garage right as we are backing out. Mom looks at me with wide eyes, she isn't talking, just gasping for air. I don't know where we are going but realize neither does Mom. She hits the gas hard and with a screech of the wheels, followed by a twist of the steering wheel, we are gone. Pets quickly gets in his car. I only know this because Mom says, 'Oh my God, he is following us.'

I am surprised he can drive in his staggering condition and wonder why he has so much motivation to chase us.

I turn around and see Pets catching up to us, very close behind. I ask Mom why she is afraid, and she says he is a hideous monster when he is drinking, and she is not sure what he will do. Mom loses him, and we take a hard right and pull over at a random fence, no houses around. Mom gets out of the car and grabs me as it seems faster. Mom realizes the fence is barb wire, and a slight panic sets in when we see Pets in the distance. We thought we lost him. Mom gets me under the barbed wire and leaps over it without scratching up her arms. We start to run as fast as we can, my four-year-old feet trying to stretch my legs to keep up. Mom is holding my hand in case I fall. I take a tiny peek behind me as I am running and see Pets just standing there, shaking his fist. The barbed wire fence gave him pause, and he was too wobbly to run across a bumpy dirt field. What would he have done had he caught us? We do not know if Pets will give up. We see an old barn with the door wide open, without any people or animals inside, just cobwebs and hay on the ground.

Mom is out of breath. We sit on a haybale for what seems like hours. I try to talk, but Mom shushes me. We need to be quiet in case the monster finds us. I look at Mom's blank face and do not say a word. It strikes me as strange that we were cleaning the house together earlier and having a nice time, that we had planned a trip to the day-old bread store for goodies, then suddenly a car chase, and now sitting quietly in a stinky barn.

I whisper to my mom, 'I hate the hideous monster.'

My mom looks over at me and doesn't say anything, just a look of sadness I will never forget. We go back home. Pets is asleep even though it is the afternoon. Cassie is still at school and Mom pretends nothing happened. We never talked about it again."

Dr. Beck responded, "Lane, you shared a difficult story of you and your mom being chased by your alcoholic stepfather. Perhaps your current situation with Max is due, in part, to feelings from when you were younger. When you were little and unable to control what was happening around you. Sometimes we can relive previous traumatic events that come up unexpectedly as in your case, when you had the miscarriage. Max could be the embodiment of you as a child, needing protection that you did not have. I am not discounting that you are hearing a little boy calling you but maybe there is a connection."

Lane thought about this for a while, not expecting her memory of being four would pop up as a connection with Max. She was not sure she agreed. Dr. Beck had Lane talk about other childhood experiences, but Lane seemed checked out once Dr. Beck mentioned she might be hearing Max because of childhood trauma. Dr. Beck sounded much more clinical and much less metaphysical than Lane expected.

"Keep your journal as experiences come up so you can share in our next session. We will try hypnosis to get a better understanding. See you next time."

Dr. Beck said this as she closed her calendar book, a signal that it was time for Lane to leave her office. Lane picked up her purse which looked more like a small duffel bag and walked out of the office, giving a nod to the tree print that looked breathless. Lane did not feel satisfied. It was true she had traumatic experiences as a child but could not believe this meant she was imagining Max.

Chapter Six

JOURNALING

In her journal entry that night, Lane was shocked by the amount of hate she had for Pets. She hated that he was not home most nights. When he did come home, he found reasons to argue with her mom so he could justify leaving to hang out at the local bar. Sometimes there was pushing and shoving, her mom often crying. Lane was only three when her mom met Pets. He never treated Lane or Cassie as his own kids. Lane felt embarrassed at school for reasons she could not understand at the time. Later, it made more sense to her. She knew her home life was not the same as others at school, but she had no way to change it. She wanted more for herself, Cassie, and her mom but the change was an impossible task for a child. She wanted to let go of the hate but holding on to it somehow felt helpful. A familiar feeling that gave her a false sense of safety against him. Pets would bang loudly on the front or back door most nights because he was too drunk to use his key. Lane wondered if Dr. Beck was right.

Perhaps her dreams merely reflected a bad childhood, surfacing intensely now because of her recent trauma. The loud banging on her back door in her dreams persisted. She had dreamed all her life of Pets banging on doors but, after the miscarriage, the banging was louder and more terrifying. These dreams were keeping her awake. Were they scaring Max? She hoped for change and wanted to give Dr. Beck a chance to help her. She hoped for a miracle.

At the next session, Lane mentioned that she journaled about Pets since their last meeting and felt a lot of hate. Dr. Beck reassured her they would work on this along with the dreams of Max. Lane was instructed to sit in the same easy chair as before and this time the easy chair would be used as a recliner. Lane would pull the lever on the side so her feet were up and another lever to make the back of the chair go down so that she was almost lying flat on her back.

At first Lane was uncomfortable, but Dr. Beck continued with several suggestive words like relax, breathe deeply, close your eyes.

Dr. Beck said, "Imagine lying down on your couch at home, you can feel the comfort of home and of the couch embracing you. I want you to remember the last time you heard Max calling you. I will count to ten slowly and you will be with Max."

Lane seemed to be in a trance; she was a good subject. Lane took several moments to go into a more relaxed state and then quickly blurted out.

"I think Max is sick. I can hear someone throwing up in my bathroom. The sound is echoing close to my bed, but Sasha doesn't startle. I hear, 'Mommy, Mommy!'" Lane almost shouted as if she were the one calling for her mother. Dr. Beck's voice turned up a notch, a sneaky dial that she turned up high or down low to suit her purpose.

"Lane, I want you to try to talk to Max. We need to know if he is OK."

Lane was silent for a minute or two.

"Lane," said Dr. Beck, "you need to follow my instructions."

Lane took a deeper breath, "I am looking for him, he is afraid, and he doesn't feel well. Someone is scaring him that also lives in my house."

"Who else lives in your house?" said Dr. Beck with a peaked curiosity. Lane replied, "I also hear a man. He is angry, yells and bangs on my back door. I don't want him to scare Max. We need to leave now."

Lane said this with a tinge of fear in her voice.

"I think it might be Pets. It sounds very much like Pets." Lane was frantic.

Dr. Beck didn't budge, as if she had Lane as her prisoner.

"Lane, I want you to ask Max who is scaring him."

"I just said, I think it's Pets." Lane said, sounding annoyed.

Lane repositioned herself nervously.

"OK, Max is here. I told him it's OK. He is with me now. Pets is scaring Max and that's why he is calling for his mommy."

"Good," said Dr. Beck, "tell him we will be needing his participation so we can help him. Ask Max why Pets is banging on the door."

Lane took a moment before responding.

"Max doesn't seem to know. He hides from him because he isn't sure what he wants."

Lane was quiet for several minutes. This seemed to bother Dr. Beck.

"Lane let's try one more time," Dr. Beck said with a stern voice.

Lane was unresponsive for several minutes; she just grinded her teeth.

Dr. Beck was frustrated as the session was going better than she had planned and she did not want it to be over. Lane would not respond. It had been 20 minutes, so Dr. Beck knew she needed to bring her out of hypnosis.

"Lane, I want you to wake up slowly, take a deep breath, relax your shoulders and open your eyes."

Lane was breathing as she was instructed to do, then she shifted her body slightly and opened her eyes. Dr. Beck reassured her that things were on track and that she was eager to help her sort out her childhood and dreams about Max in order to deal with her trauma of losing the baby. Lane felt exhausted from the session. As she was driving home, she debated if she should call her sister Cassie. Her fatigue made the decision for her and, once she was home with Sasha, she called it a day.

The next morning Lane felt refreshed but her dream the night before had been troubling, to say the least. She knew she must call Cassie right away. They shared many dreams over the years and the consensus they laughed about was that dreams were either subjective interpretation in your favor or some type of condemnation.

"Cassie, I don't remember everything from my counseling session yesterday, and you will not believe my dream last night. Max was there in full view for the first time. He cannot be more than six or seven years old. I kept saying 'Max, it's OK. I am here for you and won't let anything happen to you, ever.'"

Lane started to cry and wondered how Max could be her child if he is already six or seven? Maybe things work differently on the other side, maybe time is different. Cassie tried to compose an honest answer but didn't want to sound too negative over the phone. She was controlled, tightly wound, but also concerned about frightening Lane.

"So, you are telling me you don't remember all of the counseling session but, in your dream, you can now hang out with Max? Possibly the baby you miscarried?"

Cassie was alarmed.

"Lane, you know our childhood was messed up, but you are working with someone who may be a quack, a weirdo!! Have you checked her background? I guess I am tasked to do this for you."

Lane said nothing so as not to accept or reject Cassie's suspicions.

"Cassie, here is the clencher. I won't be sharing this with Dr. Beck because she is the one that is supposed to be figuring things out. In my dream, Pets was scaring Max. I don't know if Pets is alive or dead in real life, but it felt like Pets was banging on the back door just as he would do when we were kids. Remember? He was so drunk he couldn't fit the key in the keyhole. He could barely stand up and no matter how hard he tried it never worked so he would just start banging on the door."

"Yeah," Cassie said as she took a breath, "that was our childhood alright. I think about how much better Mom's life would have been without Pets. Nothing we can do about it now except move on, especially from your therapist."

Chapter Seven

WITH YOUR PERMISSION

Lane got herself to the next appointment; she was early, as usual. Dr. Beck practically sprung out of her office once Lane entered the waiting room. It startled Lane as if something was wrong. The session was not particularly eventful. Afterwards, as if on cue, Dr. Beck said,

"Lane, I want to do something different at our next session. With your permission, I will take you to a deeper form of hypnosis so you can be with Max. We are making great progress!"

Dr. Beck was happier than usual; generally, her tone of voice did not change, but today there was a happy spark Lane had not heard before.

"My colleague has taken a keen interest in your case. I would like for her to be present at a session in the near future, of course, with your permission. Her name is Dr. Medford."

Lane was flattered another colleague was interested and believed there must be a cure if another doctor wanted to be part of the picture.

"Sure, whatever it takes to get some sleep, thank you." Lane said in her usual timid voice. As Lane left Dr. Beck's office, she heard Dr. Beck say, "with your permission" for at least the third time and kept hearing that all the way home. Lane felt suspicion creep down her spine but could not target a reason. Lane decided she needed to call Cassie to sort it out. As Lane remembered, they had agreed she should be backing away from hypnosis. She was under the impression from the start that hypnosis was a tool with sharp edges. Although Lane had faithfully attended weekly appointments, and done hypnosis, she still had doubts.

It had crossed her mind to tell Dr. Beck that she needed a break. She had begun to feel more anxious about the sessions. Dr. Beck reassured her she was making strides in the right direction.

Lane was supposed to keep a journal and write down her dreams and conversations with Max, but Lane had started to share less and less of her journal. The next session, Lane was uncharacteristically late.

"Hi Lane, I was worried you were going to miss our session. You are a few minutes late." Lane didn't say anything as she walked into the office. Lane was oddly aware her arms were not moving as she walked, as if she were under someone's control and not walking of her own volition. Lane had a disturbing dream a few nights before that she attributed to the stress of the sessions. In this dream, Dr. Beck was conspiring with another therapist to convince her to keep Max around. In the dream Dr. Beck and her colleague were deeply interested in Max, and Lane and they were talking around a square table that made Lane feel boxed in. The only other conversation she could remember from the dream was seeing Dr. Beck wearing a dark coat which looked a little like a cloak, just as the figure in her dream before she miscarried. There were ten bubbles of light on the floor around Dr. Beck, some were as small as tennis balls and others looked like soccer balls. There was a little girl next to Dr. Beck who was staring at Lane, almost in disbelief she could see her. Lane asked if all the bubbles of light were good spirits, which again seemed to shock the little girl who could only mutter,

"I must ask Mother that question."

This haunted her but she wanted to see if the therapy sessions were bringing out the trauma of losing a baby. Maybe she was transposing this directly to Dr. Beck. However, Dr. Beck never discussed with Lane what spiritually happens to the baby when you miscarry a child, which struck Lane as odd. Perhaps that wasn't part of the therapy. Lane wondered if Dr. Beck was a believer in metaphysical things or thought about where the baby goes if it is not meant for this world. Unanswered questions kept increasing.

Chapter Eight

HOLDING ON TO MAX

As the session started, Dr. Beck seemed nervous for the first time. She was adjusting her jacket as if it were on crooked, and she arched her shoulders slightly as if she suddenly remembered she might be slouching. Lane felt ugly this day and could not figure out why. It was not the whispers of the neighbors. She could blame it on her depression from the miscarriage, but something else was in her thoughts.

Dr. Beck cleared her throat, "I am going to take you to a different time with Max, a time when you remember him enjoying his room and some of his toys."

Lane thought it peculiar that suddenly Max was an accepted part of her family, "his room and his toys."

"Now, close your eyes, breathe, think of the easy chair in your house, and, when I count to ten, you will answer everything I am asking of you. 1-2-3-4-5-6-7-8-9-10." Lane went limp and then she was speaking.

"Max is playing with an electric train from when I was a child. He loves it. There are several trains hooked together and it goes around a 3-foot circle and there is even a small light on each side. Max is playing with it; I think he keeps playing with it all night because sometimes it's still going round and round the next day."

Lane couldn't remember what else she said, only the part about the trains. Dr. Beck's head shifted slightly to the left.

"Okay, Lane." I am going to take you to a different time

in your life. A time when you were a little girl, perhaps the same age as Max. I want you to remember a time when Pets came home and you were scared. Take a deep breath, relax completely." Lane continued to another experience.

"It is really dark. My mom asked me and Cassie to run to our rooms and lock the door. We have separate bedrooms. I am by myself and hiding under my covers." Lane's breathing becomes very rapid and panicky, "Pets and Mom are screaming at each other; I don't know why he is so mean. I am scared for my mom now."

Dr. Beck went a little further. "Lane, why do you have to lock your door?"

Lane starts to cry. "Mom is scared he might hurt us."

This intrigued Dr. Beck and gave her an idea for her next session with Lane. "Ok, I need you to wake up now Lane, take a deep breath."

Lane walked out the office door, through the lobby with all its stillness and the framed tree crying for air. The fresh air outside seemed to snap her out of the session and the memories that haunted her. She picked up her step and made her way to her "old blue," what she lovingly called her slightly beat up Subaru. Lane noticed Dr. Beck's car was parked next to hers. She knew it was Dr. Beck's car because of the personalized license plate, "Beck4it," which seemed egotistical. On the other hand, maybe the license plate simply signified confidence, something Lane was searching for.

As she opened her car door, she could not help glance over, not being particularly nosey but just curious about a book Dr. Beck had on the dashboard. It was, "Where's My Baby" by Julia Rainwater. It surprised Lane, an odd title, but she shrugged it off. It wasn't her business and she had plenty else to concern her. Lane tried to stop her incessant thinking as if she needed a break from herself.

On some level Lane believed Max was the child she had miscarried. On another level, what if he was not? What if he was looking for another Mommy? Did he get tangled up at her house somehow. Her miscarriage had been traumatic, resulting in endless days wishing she could feel more normal. Her body had been in shock. A universal force took back what she had planned. Lane had been pregnant but now was without child. Lane fantasized that her physical body couldn't have a child, but the universe was helping her through the pain and sending her a baby, Max, anyway. After all, why not? Why couldn't she be the special mom that didn't really lose her baby after many weeks of fullness. The best she could do was to try not to think about it.

The following day, Lane kept looking for reasons to miss her next session, just cancel. Things had gotten more complicated, and Lane wasn't sleeping any better. She didn't have a clear picture of what was said in her sessions with Dr. Beck, which was disturbing. Also, Dr. Beck was planning on bringing another doctor to one of their sessions, without explaining why.

Lane thought of the cypress tree print at Dr Beck's office that stared at her each time she entered the waiting room. She started to feel sympathy for the tree. The crowded exposed roots around the tree, slowly suffocating. She imagined the roots rotting to a painful death if they didn't get free. Was this her fate?

Chapter Nine

The Devil in Dr. Beck

Cassie called right when Lane was contemplating canceling her next session.

"Hi Cassie, I am debating about going to my next counseling session. I am not feeling any better. Dr. Beck acts like I will get one final miraculous session at the end, which becomes less believable with each session. The timeframe is another three weeks."

Lane said this quietly as if someone else might hear the conversation. Cassie said firmly, "Lane, you need to stop going, simple as that. The point is to feel better, not worse. When was the last time you left your house to do something fun? You seem tired and your therapist sounds a little off. You need to move on."

Lane nodded her head in agreement as if Cassie could see her. She took a few moments to respond.

"I had a great dream about Max last night. We spent time together. We looked at the toys in his room and, when I woke up, I was in his room, as if I walked there in the night."

Lane was quiet again for a moment, as if she was thinking of what to say next, hoping not to sound crazy. Cassie responded with worry in her voice.

"Oh my God, the point is to let him go, not keep him around like he lives in the baby's room. It's not his room Lane. It is set up in case you have a real baby. This is terrible. I'm going to see if I can book a flight and come stay with you.

This is really disturbing."

Lane was listening to Cassie but felt incoherent. She was so tired from sleepless nights. She could only muster a tiny voice that echoed with doubt followed with an edge of "leave me alone."

"No, it's fine. Really, I am fine."

Cassie replied with suspicion, "I am going to do some research on Dr. Beck this weekend, maybe I can dig something up to convince you to end this madness."

Lane had an appointment with Dr. Beck in a few days and she was trying to sort out what to do. It seemed normal that she wouldn't remember a counseling session due to being hypnotized, but she was concerned there was more Dr. Beck should be sharing with her. Dr. Beck kept saying, "You will be amazed how much better you will feel after our sessions are completed."

It was a promise that Lane started to feel Dr. Beck couldn't deliver, even though she seemed sincere in wanting to make this happen. It seemed like a promise from someone who lived her life promising a better day that never comes.

At her next session, she was on time and Dr. Beck had a smile on her face as if saying she was feeling great regardless of Lane not doing any better. They did the usual routine of Lane going under hypnosis. Then, Dr. Beck got greedy and seemed to abuse her metaphysical approach in a curious way.

"Lane, I want to see if we can connect with the mother of Max. We know this may be a possibility."

Lane agreed and was put into a deep hypnotic state.

"Max is calling for Mommy. I go to him, but he is pointing in the corner of the room. His mother doesn't say her name, but somehow I feel it is his mommy, 'LoLo.' She is blocked from entering, as if a door that should easily open is broken. She is unable to open it but is holding up a key. She is telling me I need to open the door. I need to set Max free. She has been looking for Max and wants to bring him home."

At this point Dr. Beck has an open mouth and can barely contain herself. She looked like a dog drooling on herself. She dug deeper because this was too good to be true.

"Lane, we need to ask Lolo how we can open the door for her to get Max." Lane remained quiet for several minutes.

"Max is not the baby I miscarried; I need to say goodbye. I will release the hate that is allowing Pets to be around my house so I can open the door for Max to go home. Pets scared me as a child and now he has scared Max to the point he is afraid to go through the door. I will set him free."

"Why so sudden Lane? Just a few more sessions please, ask him to stay." Lane was unresponsive for a very long time.

Dr. Beck knew she had to bring her out of hypnosis, but she didn't want to. Eventually, she did.

Chapter Ten

Dr. Beck, Searching for Elizabeth

D r. Beck was having breakfast in her usual kitchen nook on the west wing of her estate. She lived large, her house, which resembled a mansion, was left to her by her parents. She had many visitors. Now in her late 50s, she wanted to do something different with her life. In a material sense, she had everything and anything she needed but wasn't especially grateful. She knew nothing other than a life of hired help, including nannies, when she was young, private schools and college, and connections that helped her become a doctor. Dr. Beck had a medical degree, but she never remembered her parents asking her if that was her life choice.

Once her parents died, she pursued her lifelong dream as a writer. Her interest was women. Specifically, women who had emotional experiences arising from a miscarriage. She had miscarried a child after a brief relationship with a fellow doctor in medical school. Afterwards, she and her boyfriend turned on each other. Each thought the other had not properly prepared for this life changing event. This experience changed her life, and the relationship ended in devastation and disappointment. This continued to haunt Dr. Beck. She wrote a few short articles in medical school about dreams she had of her miscarried child, a little girl Dr. Beck named Elizabeth.

It seemed Dr. Beck was unconsciously trying to figure out her own story through this experience with Lane.

However, Lane was more like a victim in this arrangement. Lane was not getting any better and Dr. Beck did not care. Dr. Beck was running a scam and invited women by posting an ad in local papers to share their grief and tell their stories of miscarrying a child. It was something she initially tried in an experimental way with little success and results remained unsatisfactory. The women were either reluctant to come forward with their pain or Dr. Beck did not find their stories sufficiently intriguing. Lane presented neither of these deficiencies, but this only proved that Dr. Beck wasn't prepared for a woman who had an extraordinary story to tell. It was a story she wanted to get on tape and turn into a novel. For Lane, this was a wrong turn. Instead of trying to learn from and solve Lane's predicament, Dr. Beck was consumed with counseling Lane, continuing the hypnosis, and getting a story. She was intent on keeping alive the possibility in Lane's mind, whether she believed it or not, that Max was Lane's miscarried child. It occupied her thoughts daily. If she could figure this out with Lane, perhaps she could resolve her pain from her miscarried child, Elizabeth, as well as get a book. A hope she had been having for years.

Before the next session started, Dr. Beck told Lane,

"Dr. Medford is going to observe our session, with your permission."

Dr. Medford was a large woman with eyes equally large. She kept staring at Lane without talking. Lane wondered if she ever blinked. There was a heaviness around her that made Lane feel small.

"Okay, I am ready."

In an earlier conversation by phone Dr. Beck had with Dr. Medford, Dr. Beck explained that Lane was starting to spontaneously channel other energies when she was under hypnosis. The sessions started with Lane talking to Max, a spirit in her house. Max was hiding from someone or something and now he was looking for his mommy. It was never clear if Lane was his mommy or if Max was lost and another mommy was out there. What startled Dr. Beck was now someone named Lolo was coming through, asking for Max.

Lane quickly went under hypnosis. There had been many such sessions and they grew more intense once Lolo was revealed. Dr. Beck had mentioned this briefly to Lane but didn't go in to too much detail.

"Lane, I want you to try and connect with either Lolo or someone on the other side who can tell us how to help Max."

A bright light was in front of Lane, elevating her to what seemed like a sacred place full of sparks of light.

"A beautiful warrior angel is in front of me. He has a message."

Immediately, Lane's voice changed, channeling this other entity.

"You are mothering a spirit child in your mortal world. This is not recommended. Your spirit child is very powerful. He is not a bad spirit but has many powers. He bumped another spirit meant for your world out of place, out of pure mischievous fun. It was an **ACCIDENTAL CROSSING.** A child spirit disrupting the order, even by accident, is dangerous. Especially a spirit raised to simultaneously exist in both worlds. Others are looking to take advantage of his innocence and advance him in the wrong spiritual direction, possibly harming others. It was not his time to be on Earth. He has much to learn on our side before getting the free rein he has secured under your care. If you continue to raise him until he becomes a man, his power will be corrupted.

He already has a spirit posing as a father. It is time for you to say goodbye to Max. He came to you as a sickly child because he was lost and knew this would motivate you to continue caring for him. Again, he is not a bad spirit, just misguided. It is time to say goodbye."

Lane's facial expression changed dramatically, and she seemed distressed. Dr. Medford and Dr. Beck smiled with delight, as if two devils met up for a sweet feast.

"Lane, we have more questions for the angel warrior, ask him not to leave."

Lane repositioned herself in the recliner, "He is gone."

Dr. Beck blurted out, "Wait, do not do that yet, there is much we need to learn."

At that moment, there was a loud banging sound at the door that snapped Lane out of her hypnosis. It was Cassie. She had made the long journey and was frantic.

"Lane," Cassie was shouting, "Let's go!"

Lane stumbled to her feet. Dr. Beck yelled, "No, get back." She was trying to block Cassie from grabbing Lane's arm to pull her out of the office recliner. Dr. Beck seemed not only desperate but mean as she yelled,

"This is my patient and you have disrupted her condition!"

Lane had a blank look on her face. Cassie said,

"I will call the police if you don't let her walk out of the room."

Dr. Beck's demeanor changed almost immediately, as if embarrassed and said "Who are you?" Cassie stared at Dr. Beck with a look resembling an animal protecting its own.

"I am her sister, her family."

"Well, this is rather rude," said Dr. Beck. "I have never had this happen before."

Cassie and Lane exited the last door and got out of the building. Dr. Beck was almost mumbling at this point but came out and said,

"I will be in touch with you Lane."

Dr. Beck said it sneakily as if to imply she would save Lane from Cassie. Cassie was unable to speak until they got in the car.

"Lane, Dr. Beck is not who you think. I found out she lost her medical degree years ago for inappropriate behavior. She is now a writer but poses as a medical doctor to get subjects. She has a lot of complaints about her, women that she has hurt psychologically. I found out she uses a fake name when she writes about miscarriages and spirits. She lures women to talk about it by saying she is a specialist in post trauma and a metaphysical person. It is all a hoax. I found out her mom had several miscarriages and, at one point in her childhood, Dr. Beck was briefly institutionalized for talking to what she said were her siblings that had crossed over. It wasn't easy to find all this, but, once I was hot on her trail, I could not believe it and I had to make sure you weren't imprisoned by her madness."

Lane was shaking. Things had changed so quickly. She had been caught up in someone's mess!

That night, after an exhausting conversation with Cassie to rehash the events of the day, everyone, including Sasha and probably Max, were ready to call it a night.

Chapter Eleven

SAYING GOODBYE TO MAX

L ane remembered every word the warrior angel had said, an out of body experience she would never forget.

Lane woke up in the middle of the night from a deep sleep or so she thought. A bright light was in front of her, again elevating her to what seemed like a sacred place full of sparks of light. Lane knew what she needed to do. She felt clarity and understanding, which brought much needed relief. She felt happy for the first time since she could remember. She felt lighter thanks to the energy of, and conversation with, the angel warrior. She would say goodbye to Max. She had not given birth to Max, but he was a child and she had loved and she cared for him. Just as Lane was having these thoughts, Max appeared in full view. He was a seven-year-old boy with gentle features and a smile that could light up any room. Lane sat next to Max on a small chair and hugged him, and they were communicating without exchanging words. They felt their love for each other. Just as they were trying to say sorry, Max for bumping a child out of line and Lane for hanging on to Max for fear he was the child she was meant to parent, these thoughts disappeared.

Love filled their hearts. Lane would later tell Cassie this love could last her a lifetime. This connection was so spectacular, as if the universe hushed for a few moments to see the sparks of two galaxies coming together to make right what was wrong. It lit up the sky in Lolo's village. That was the moment they knew the passage for Max to return was open and Lane had to act quickly. The dark energy and the loud banging she would hear most nights on her back door had stopped. The door blocking Max to get back home was open. Lane would secure Max's travel home.

A gentle tug pulled Max away to what looked like a long hallway, a hallway full of beautiful colors sprinkled as far down the hall as one could see. Lolo was off in the distance, finally able to bring her child home. Lane could see her but not actually touch her as she could Max. Lolo smiled openly to Lane. One of understanding, relief, and love. Lane was crying. It was the first time she knew how it felt to love a child unconditionally, to be willing to do anything for them. Lane knew she would miss Max and expected to see him again. In any case, the only thing that mattered was that he was home with his mom, Lolo.

Chapter Twelve

Max is Home, Lolo's Thoughts.

As the silent calm of the late evening gently wrapped around Lolo's shoulders, she felt instant comfort. As she stood on her front porch, a whisper surrounded her, and she looked up to see if the wind or trees were trying to get her attention. The tall trees appeared to be waiting for her to say something, a gesture or maybe a scream. The trees had always been her companions. They waited with her for this day, reassuring and perhaps forgiving her. Now it was night, the dark had come quickly. She could see the fireflies bouncing around as if in celebration. The easy stillness for just a few moments in time invited her to quiet her thoughts and reflect on all the craziness of the previous year.

Max was finally home, after much heartache and searching. She looked over at Max, sound asleep on the porch swing covered by his favorite fuzzy blanket embroidered with the galaxy patterns he loved so much to read about. The mom that held on to Max in her grief of losing a child was the same mom who made sure he could make the journey home. Lolo had heard about the accidental crossing from Scottie. He came to her hut to tell her personally because Max had been under his care. Lolo wept for days, begging with those who could help her. It appeared the tunnel Max fell through was sealed after he fell, and it took time to find an alternative. Unbeknownst to Lolo and Lane, they had been grieving the loss of a child together. It was this grief that had eventually connected them and brought Max back.

Chapter Thirteen

THREE YEARS LATER

Lane and Sasha were getting ready for their morning routine of walking to Mo's coffee house. The past three years had been a healing time for Lane. She and her sister reported Dr. Beck to the authorities, hoping to end Dr. Beck's deceitfulness, or at least slow her down. Lane had been disturbed by the woman she saw crying at Dr. Beck's office, but when she asked Dr. Beck about it, she said it was because the girl had changed her mind about counseling. Lane knew it was likely Dr. Beck was no longer interested in her because she was not providing enough "material." Lane had reported to the medical board that Dr. Beck was selfishly using her medical degree to lure innocent women in need of help. In fact, Dr. Beck had stopped practicing as a therapist a decade ago. She had a pen name and had published a few books which were unsuccessful.

Unbeknownst to Dr. Medford, who was Dr. Beck's publisher, Lane was a patient and Dr. Beck was still actively "treating" patients. She had become close with Dr. Beck over the years and thought she was supporting Dr. Beck in her second career as a writer. Dr. Beck told her Lane wanted a ghost writer for her story, nothing more. It was obvious Lane had a lot to say from her dreams and hypnotic sessions. Dr. Beck had wanted a witness, namely her publisher, for what she felt was jackpot material for a best selling novel.

Lane sat in the usual patio area at Mo's and got a copy of the community paper. She had joined a Yoga class and met a couple friends there, which helped her mood. This also helped Cassie to not worry about her. Lane was working part time from home doing teaching plans for kids who were home schooled for a high school engineering class. Lane was glowing. She put a flower behind her ear that she found mysteriously growing in her otherwise barren front porch. Sasha was asleep, as usual. Lane took a deep breath as she positioned herself to slowly take a sip of her latte before calling Cassie. The sounds of George Winston's music played gently from the patio speakers at Mo's. Whenever she heard George Winston's music, it made her happy. The timing of the music was perfect and she felt the universe was smiling with her. Cassie answered the phone and, before she could say hello, Lane blurted, "I'm pregnant!" Those two words echoed for several seconds. They could not see one another, but they both had smiles and watery eyes. Her baby's name would be Oliver if a boy, Sophia if a girl.

About the Author

Laura Barnett received a Master's Degree in Rehabilitation Counseling from San Francisco State University. Laura lives in the Bay Area with her husband Rob and two children, Nick and Alec. She has nurtured her passion for writing this story for many years.

ABOOKS

ALIVE Book Publishing and ALIVE Publishing Group
are imprints of Advanced Publishing LLC,
3200 A Danville Blvd., Suite 204, Alamo, California 94507

Telephone: 925.837.7303
alivebookpublishing.com

Printed by BoD™in Norderstedt, Germany

9 781631 321986